Lester and the Bear

by Nancy Nielsen

ISBN 0-15-313953-6

Ordering Options
ISBN 0-15-314006-2 (Grade 6 Collection)
ISBN 0-15-314160-3 (package of 5)

1 2 3 4 5 6 7 8 9 10 026 99 98

Jake left the house quietly and headed toward the
kennel. It was a crisp October morning. The sun was not
yet up.

Jake's faithful dog, Lester, greeted Jake with a few
excited yelps. He knew why the boy was there. Jake
opened the kennel door. Then the two started up the trail
for their morning walk.

The two friends walked a mile or so up the trail. The rising sun began to warm them. It was going to be a sunny day. Jake whistled a tune. Lester darted after a movement he saw in the bushes.

"Hey, Lester, what'd you find there?" Jake called to his dog. Lester was sniffing in a small hole filled with leaves. Jake kicked at the leaves. There seemed to be nothing there except a piece of bark from a birch tree. Lester, however, continued to bark and sniff.

"You're only after a piece of tree bark," Jake said to Lester. He picked up the bark. Then he saw what was under it. "It's just an old, discarded can!" he said aloud.

Jake noticed bits of black fur on the mouth of the can. Then he stuffed the discarded can into his backpack. "I wish people would take their garbage home with them. Animals can get cut on cans," he grumbled aloud.

Lester was sniffing along a path off to the left. "Okay, Lester," Jake said. "We'll go this way today." They started up the trail.

They hiked along the trail for a while. Jake's stomach rumbled. He decided to stop for a snack near a stream.

The water in the stream sparkled from the sun's rays. Except for the sound of the water, the forest was quiet. Lester also became quiet and still. Then he whined.

"What's the matter, Lester?" Jake asked. He looked over at Lester. The dog was crouched on the ground, frightened. He let out a couple of whimpers.

Then Jake looked up. A huge black bear stood silently on the trail ahead. It was sniffing the air. Then it growled and came toward Jake.

Lester snarled, jumped up, and ran toward the bear. "No, Lester!" Jake cried. "You're too small to take on a bear!"

It was too late. The bear took a swipe at Lester. One huge paw swept the small dog into the air. Lester landed with a thud in a heap of leaves. Then the bear ran off into the woods.

Jake ran over to Lester. Gently he caressed the brave dog's head. There were ugly scratches on Lester's side. Blood was soaking the dog's fur.

Lester whimpered as Jake wrapped his beloved dog in his jacket and picked him up. He carried Lester all the way into town. He took the wounded dog to the only person who might be able to save him.

"His wounds are serious," the vet said. "You'll have to leave him here overnight."

"He saved my life," said Jake.

"And you saved his," replied the doctor. "You're both lucky."

The next day, Lester looked much better. He stood up, wagged his tail, and barked.

"Keep him quiet for a few days," said the vet. "Then bring him back, and I'll remove the stitches."

Jake hugged Lester. His brave friend was going home.

Follow the Trail

On the map, draw a line to show the walk Jake and Lester took. Place an X where they met the bear. Draw another line to show how Jake probably got to the vet's clinic.

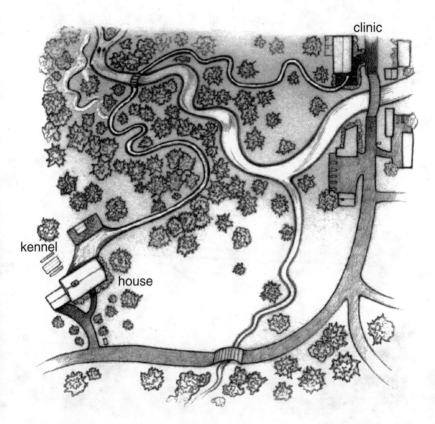

You can check your answer on the back of this book.

TAKE-HOME BOOK